# WINGS OF FIRE

## THE DARK SECRET
### THE GRAPHIC NOVEL

For Oscar and Beatrice, two of the most awesome
people ever — we feel so lucky to have you as friends!
—T.T.S.

For Ruby and Gabby, who I hope will always
let me know if my art's any good
—M.H.

Story and text copyright © 2021 by Tui T. Sutherland
Adaptation by Barry Deutsch and Rachel Swirsky
Map and border design © 2012 by Mike Schley
Art by Mike Holmes © 2021 by Scholastic Inc.

Library of Congress Control Number Available

ISBN 978-1-338-34422-6 (hardcover)
ISBN 978-1-338-34421-9 (paperback)

10 9 8 7 6 5 4 3 2 1          21 22 23 24 25

Printed in China   62
First edition, January 2021
Edited by Amanda Maciel
Coloring by Maarta Laiho
Lettering by E.K. Weaver
Creative Director: Phil Falco
Publisher: David Saylor

# WINGS OF FIRE

## THE DARK SECRET
### THE GRAPHIC NOVEL

BY TUI T. SUTHERLAND

ADAPTED BY BARRY DEUTSCH
AND RACHEL SWIRSKY

ART BY MIKE HOLMES
COLOR BY MAARTA LAIHO

AN IMPRINT OF
SCHOLASTIC

Queen Scarlet's
Palace

Diamond Spray River

Diamond Spray
Delta

Kingdom of
the Sea

Mud Kingdom

Scavenger Den

Scavenger
Den

Rainforest Kingdom

THE DARK SECRET

# THE DRAGONET PROPHECY

WHEN THE WAR HAS LASTED TWENTY YEARS...
THE DRAGONETS WILL COME.
WHEN THE LAND IS SOAKED IN BLOOD AND TEARS...
THE DRAGONETS WILL COME.

FIND THE SEAWING EGG OF DEEPEST BLUE.
WINGS OF NIGHT SHALL COME TO YOU.

THE LARGEST EGG IN MOUNTAIN HIGH
WILL GIVE TO YOU THE WINGS OF SKY.

FOR WINGS OF EARTH, SEARCH THROUGH THE MUD
FOR AN EGG THE COLOR OF DRAGON BLOOD.
AND HIDDEN ALONE FROM THE RIVAL QUEENS,
THE SANDWING EGG AWAITS UNSEEN.

Of three queens who blister and blaze and burn
Two shall die and one shall learn
If she bows to a fate that is stronger and higher,
She'll have the power of wings of fire.

Five eggs to hatch on brightest night,
Five dragons born to end the fight.
Darkness will rise to bring the light.
The dragonets are coming...

REED, I HATE THIS WAR!

I DON'T UNDERSTAND WHAT WE'RE FIGHTING FOR. WHO CARES WHO THE SANDWING QUEEN IS? WHY AM I FIGHTING AN ICEWING OVER A THRONE THAT HAS NOTHING TO DO WITH EITHER OF US?

QUEEN MOORHEN MUST HAVE A GOOD REASON FOR ALLYING WITH BURN AND THE SKYWINGS, UMBER. WE SHOULDN'T DOUBT HER.

BESIDES, THE WAR WILL BE OVER SOON. CLAY IS GOING TO END IT.

THAT'S TRUE, SORA! CLAY AND HIS FRIENDS WILL SAVE US.

DO THEY WISH CLAY WAS LEADING THEM INSTEAD OF ME?

WHY WOULD ICEWINGS EVEN BE SCOUTING AROUND HERE?

MAYBE THEY WERE HERE FOR THE SCAVENGER DEN, MARSH.

WHAT SCAVENGER DEN?

YOU DIDN'T SMELL IT? WE FLEW RIGHT OVER IT.

WHY WOULD ICEWINGS CARE ABOUT A SCAVENGER DEN?

IT DOESN'T MATTER. WHAT MATTERS IS THAT WE SURVIVED ANOTHER BATTLE, THANKS TO REED.

I HOPE WE SURVIVE THE *NEXT* ONE.

I HOPE CLAY FULFILLS THE PROPHECY AND ENDS THE WAR BEFORE WE HAVE TO DO ANY MORE FIGHTING.

I HOPE SO, TOO.

BEFORE THIS WAR TAKES ANYONE ELSE I CARE ABOUT.

# PART ONE: THE SECRET PLAN

WHERE AM I? WHERE ARE MY FRIENDS?

IS SUNNY OKAY?

EVERYTHING IS FUZZY... I CAN'T REMEMBER...

MAYBE I DREAMED IT ALL. MAYBE WE'RE STILL UNDER THE MOUNTAIN AND IT WAS ALL A NIGHTMARE.

NO, I *COULDN'T* HAVE MADE UP MORROWSEER.

NIGHTWINGS HAVE A REPUTATION TO UPHOLD. YOU MUST MAKE THE OTHERS FEAR AND FOLLOW YOU, OR YOU'LL BE THE GREATEST DISAPPOINTMENT IN NIGHTWING HISTORY.

OR THE RAINFOREST... THAT'S WHERE I WAS, WHEN SOMETHING...

I THINK THERE'S SOMETHING WRONG WITH HIM.

MAYBE THEY KILLED HIM. THAT'D BE ALL RIGHT. THEN *I* CAN BE IN THE PROPHECY INSTEAD.

WON'T YOU GET SICK?

NIGHTWINGS DON'T *GET* SICK.

DON'T TELL ME YOU HAVE A WEAK STOMACH IN ADDITION TO EVERYTHING *ELSE* WRONG WITH YOU.

NO, BUT... THERE'S PROBABLY HORRIBLE BACTERIA ALL THROUGH THAT WOUND.

OF COURSE. HOW DO YOU THINK IT DIED? MY BITE INFECTED IT.

THIS ISN'T HOW YOU HUNT, TOO?

USUALLY CLAY AND TSUNAMI HUNT FOR ALL OF US.

BUT I'VE NEVER SEEN ANY DRAGON HUNT LIKE THIS. HOW DOES IT WORK?

YOU BITE YOUR PREY AND THEN WAIT FOR IT TO DIE. AND YOU EAT IT ONCE IT'S ALREADY DEAD AND ROTTING.

SOMETHING IN YOUR MOUTH KILLS THEM, EVEN IF THE BITE ITSELF WASN'T FATAL. IS IT VENOM?

SOME OF OUR SCIENTISTS THINK SO, BUT THEY HAVEN'T FOUND ANY EVIDENCE.

HERE.

UH. NO, THANK YOU.

WHAT DO YOU THINK YOU'RE GOING TO EAT? THIS IS THE NIGHTWING WAY.

I'LL CATCH SOMETHING ELSE. A LIZARD OR SOMETHING.

YOU KNOW, WE ALL ASSUMED YOU'D BE BORN NATURALLY SUPERIOR, LIKE OTHER NIGHTWINGS. BUT NO. APPARENTLY YOU'RE DEFECTIVE.

WELL, WE DON'T HAVE TIME FOR YOUR DELICATE SENSIBILITIES. EAT THE WING OR STARVE.

LISTEN, IT MIGHT NOT MAKE YOU SICK, BUT I THINK IT WOULD MAKE *ME* SICK.

I'M NOT USED TO EATING INFECTED CARRION. SCIENTIFICALLY I WOULD ASSUME IT'S SOMETHING YOU ADJUST TO OVER TIME, AS YOUR DRAGONETS WILL HAVE DONE. BUT *I* WON'T HAVE THE CORRECT ANTIBODIES TO KEEP ME SAFE.

WELL, THAT ANSWERS THAT QUESTION.

WHAT QUESTION?

NOW I KNOW WHO YOUR FATHER IS.

THIS IS ALL SO *DRAB.* NOT LIKE THE OTHER DRAGON KINGDOMS I'VE SEEN.

I GUESS NO ONE EVER COMES HERE. INSTEAD OF TRYING TO IMPRESS OTHER DRAGONS WITH OPULENCE, THEY DO IT WITH MYSTERY.

DID I HEAR TALONSTEPS?

MAYBE IT'S GLORY, COMING TO RESCUE ME! OR CLAY!

IF CLAY RESCUES ME NOW, I PROMISE I WILL NEVER, EVER MAKE FUN OF HIM AGAIN.

I KNOW! I HEARD YOU.

BUT I *GOT* BORED, AND SAW YOU FLYING BY, SO I THOUGHT I'D COME, TOO!

I'M *FINALLY* IN THE NIGHTWING PALACE! I'VE HAD SO *MANY* PROPHETIC DREAMS ABOUT IT!

ALTHOUGH I MUST SAY, IN MY VISIONS IT WAS BIGGER AND LIGHTER AND SMELLED *WAY* LESS TERRIBLE; PLUS, IT HAD A *LOT* MORE TREASURE AND *SERIOUSLY* FEWER GRUMPY DRAGONS.

HM. MAYBE THOSE WERE JUST NORMAL DREAMS.

FATESPEAKER. WHAT DID I SAY ABOUT KEEPING YOUR VISIONS TO YOURSELF?

YOU SAID, "SHUT UP ABOUT YOUR VISIONS. I'M NOT EVEN REMOTELY INTERESTED."

BUT THAT DOESN'T MEAN *THIS* DRAGON ISN'T INTERESTED! YOU'RE INTERESTED, AREN'T YOU?

UH—

ANYWAY!

I KNOW YOU'RE IMPORTANT AND WE SHARE AN AMAZING DESTINY TOGETHER AND—

GO BACK TO YOUR CAVE.

OH, CAN'T I *GO* WITH YOU? I FORESEE THAT I'LL BE REALLY, REALLY HELPFUL AT WHATEVER YOU'RE ABOUT TO DO! AND ALSO THAT I'LL FIND IT TOTALLY INTERESTING.

I'M NOT SURE THAT COUNTS AS FORESEEING.

SUCH A HANDSOME DRAGONET. SO HEALTHY AND STRONG. HE DOES LOOK LIKE ME! I KNEW HE WOULD. THIS JAWLINE IS DOMINANT.

AH, AND YES, SEE THE WAY THE SCALES ON OUR WINGS SPRAY OUTWARD, LIKE A SPLASH OF WATER.

A LARGER DATA SET WOULD NATURALLY BE ESSENTIAL FOR PROVING ANYTHING, BUT ONE IS MUCH BETTER THAN NONE; ENTIRELY WONDERFUL, IN FACT, COMPARED TO MOST OF THE TRIBE.

UGH.

INCLUDING YOURSELF, MORROWSEER, RIGHT? NO DRAGONETS AS OF YET, *HMM?*

BUT I HAVE A SON! I OF ALL DRAGONS! YOU CAN BE MY ASSISTANT. WHAT ARE YOU INTERESTED IN, SON?

*SON.*

UM, EVERYTHING. SCROLLS? I LIKE SCROLLS.

*FANTASTIC!* I HAVE LOTS OF SCROLLS.

OUR UNDERSTANDING OF THIS BIOLOGICAL ANOMALY IS SO NEW THAT WE HAVEN'T EVEN PUT IT IN ANY SCROLLS. IT TURNS OUT ONE TRIBE OF DRAGONS HAS EVOLVED AN UNUSUAL DEFENSE MECHANISM. YOU'LL NEVER GUESS WHICH ONE!

OH NO.

RAINWINGS!

RAINWINGS?

YES! THEY CAN SHOOT *VENOM* FROM THEIR *FANGS!* LET ME SHOW YOU.

ONE OF OUR FIRST QUESTIONS, NATURALLY, WAS HOW FAR CAN THEY SHOOT? WHAT'S A SAFE DISTANCE TO ATTACK THEM FROM?

THIS IS AS FAR AS I'VE EVER SEEN A DRAGON SHOOT. AN OLDER MALE, SUGGESTING THE SKILL GETS STRONGER AS THEY AGE.

THE NEXT QUESTION, OF COURSE, WAS WHAT *DOESN'T* REACT TO THE VENOM? WHAT COULD WE USE FOR PROTECTION? METAL, FOR ONE THING.

CLANG

CLANG

BUT ANYTHING BIOLOGICAL, IT DESTROYS.

EWW!

IF IT GETS IN YOUR EYES OR YOUR BLOOD-STREAM, YOU'RE DEAD, ALMOST INSTANTLY. IF IT HITS YOUR SCALES, YOU ONLY WISH YOU WERE.

I *KNOW* WHAT IT CAN DO. I'VE SEEN IT KILL TWO DRAGONS.

THREE, IF QUEEN SCARLET IS DEAD.

TWO, REALLY? HOW SURPRISINGLY CARELESS. WE HAVEN'T PICKED UP ANY RAINWINGS WITH THAT LITTLE CONTROL YET.

IT WASN'T "CARELESS." IT WAS ON PURPOSE.

ON *PURPOSE?* THAT CHANGES THINGS ENTIRELY! I WANT TO KNOW EVERYTHING! HOW LONG DID DEATH TAKE, WHAT PROMPTED THE ATTACK—

I SHOULDN'T HAVE SAID ANYTHING—I SHOULDN'T LET THEM KNOW GLORY CAN BE DANGEROUS.

I THOUGHT RAINWINGS NEVER ATTACKED OTHER DRAGONS.

EVEN A RAINWING WILL DEFEND HERSELF SOMETIMES.

IN MY EXPERIENCE, NOT OFTEN.

BUT WHY DON'T YOU STAND BACK JUST IN CASE.

WHAT ARE YOU *DOING* TO HER?!

WE WERE TESTING TO SEE WHETHER THEY RUN OUT OF VENOM AT SOME POINT. BUT SHE FAINTED BEFORE WE COULD GET ANY REALLY USEFUL DATA.

I MUST ATTEND MY DAILY MEETING WITH THE QUEEN. WE WILL CATCH UP SOON, WON'T WE? IT WAS FANTASTIC TO MEET YOU! I AM SO VERY PROUD!

WOW.

SO... TURNS OUT WE MIGHT BE *HORRIBLE.* I DID *NOT* FORESEE THAT AT ALL.

I BELIEVED EVERYTHING I READ—ABOUT NIGHTWINGS BEING SO NOBLE AND BRILLIANT AND PERFECT. I CAN'T UNDERSTAND THIS.

YOU'RE NOT HORRIBLE, THOUGH. WHY ARE YOU DIFFERENT FROM THE OTHERS? WHERE HAVE YOU BEEN?

I WAS RAISED BY THE TALONS OF PEACE, TOO.

WHAT? I NEVER SAW YOU IN THE CAMP!

WE WERE KEPT HIDDEN UNDER A MOUNTAIN. UH. ACTUALLY... *I'M* THE DRAGONET IN THE PROPHECY.

OR I *WAS.* I GUESS YOU'RE MY REPLACEMENT.

WHAT?!

WHY ARE THEY TORTURING THE RAINWINGS? I CAN FIGURE THIS OUT.

MAYBE THEY WANT TO USE RAINWING VENOM THEMSELVES? THEY'RE ON QUEEN BLISTER'S SIDE. MAYBE THEY'LL USE RAINWING VENOM TO FIGHT FOR HER?

BUT WHY WOULD THEY JOIN NOW, EIGHTEEN YEARS INTO THE WAR?

PERHAPS BLISTER PROMISED THE NIGHTWINGS SOMETHING, THE WAY BLAZE IS GIVING UP TERRITORY TO THE ICEWINGS IN EXCHANGE FOR THEIR HELP.

**TERRITORY!**
MORE THAN ANYTHING, THE NIGHTWINGS NEED A NEW HOME. THE ISLAND IS A *HORRIBLE* PLACE TO LIVE, AND THE VOLCANO IS EXTREMELY DANGEROUS.

MASTERMIND'S EXPERIMENTS ARE ALL ABOUT HOW TO DEFEND AGAINST RAINWING VENOM BECAUSE *THE NIGHTWINGS ARE PLANNING TO INVADE THE RAINFOREST!*

*THAT'S* WHAT BLISTER PROMISED THEM. IF THE NIGHTWINGS HELP BLISTER WIN THE WAR, BLISTER WILL USE HER ARMIES AND MAGIC TUNNEL FROM THE DESERT TO HELP THE NIGHTWINGS DESTROY THE RAINWINGS.

THINK, STARFLIGHT, THINK!

AND *I'M* THE ONLY ONE WHO KNOWS. BUT I'M... I'M NOT BRAVE OR STRONG. HOW CAN *I* SAVE THE RAINWINGS? HOW DO I STOP MY OWN TRIBE?

I THINK HE WENT IN HERE!

GET HIM!

HEY! STOP!

I CAN'T HELP THIS POOR RAINWING RIGHT NOW—I'VE GOT TO *HIDE!*

WHERE IS HE?

INTRUDERS! A SKYWING! AND A MUDWING!

THE GUARD MUST HAVE SOME SORT OF ALARM GONG.

BOOONG!

BOOONG!

BOOONG!

STOP THAT! WE'RE SUPPOSED TO BE HERE!

WE'RE HERE TO KILL A NIGHTWING DRAGONET! WHERE'D HE GO?

WOW. *THAT* WAS THE WRONG THING TO SAY.

THEY'RE HERE TO KILL OUR DRAGONETS! GET THEM!

WHACK! SMASH! OUCH!

LEGGO! WHAM! SMACK!

SOUNDS LIKE MORE GUARDS HAVE ARRIVED.

MORROWSEER HAS BEEN TRYING TO HAVE GLORY KILLED SINCE THE FIRST MOMENT HE SAW HER. BECAUSE SHE'S A RAINWING, AND HE'S AFRAID SHE'LL FIGURE OUT HIS PLAN AND WARN HER TRIBE.

HE *DOESN'T* THINK GLORY'S WEAK AND USELESS. HE'S WORRIED ABOUT WHAT SHE MIGHT DO.

AS HE *SHOULD* BE.

QUIET UP THERE... I THINK FLAME AND OCHRE HAVE BEEN DRAGGED OFF. I HOPE VIPER AND SQUID MET A SIMILAR FATE. JUST IN CASE, I'D BETTER STAY HIDDEN AWHILE.

I COULD TRY TO ESCAPE, GET BACK TO THE RAINFOREST TO WARN GLORY.

BUT SURELY THE TUNNEL'S GUARDED. AND IF I GET CAUGHT TRYING TO WARN GLORY, MORROWSEER WILL KILL ME HIMSELF.

STARFLIGHT? IT'S ME, FATESPEAKER.

IT'S GOING TO TAKE SOME EXPLAINING TO GET FLAME AND OCHRE OUT OF THE DUNGEON.

THAT WAS A VERY CLEVER WAY TO FOIL YOUR ATTACKERS, STARFLIGHT. IT'S NOT WHAT I'D HAVE DONE, BUT IT WORKED.

WHETHER YOU *INTENDED* IT OR NOT.

FATESPEAKER, IT SEEMS LIKE *YOU* HAD AN OPPORTUNITY TO KILL HIM AND DIDN'T TAKE IT.

LOOK, DESTINY IS DESTINY.

I DON'T SEE WHY YOU'RE SO WORRIED ABOUT THE PROPHECY. YOU DELIVERED IT—NOW YOU CAN SIT BACK AND WATCH IT HAPPEN. WHETHER IT'S ME OR STARFLIGHT, WHO CARES?

THE NIGHTWINGS CARE. THE QUEEN HAS DECREED I SHOULD CHOOSE ONE OF YOU AND KILL THE OTHER.

REALLY?

OH, POOR FATESPEAKER. HOW ARE WE BOTH GOING TO GET OUT OF THIS ALIVE?

ARE WE GOING SOMEWHERE?

DID YOU SEE THE PART OF THE FORTRESS THAT LOOKED LIKE IT COLLAPSED? I WANT TO SEE WHAT IT LOOKS LIKE FROM THE INSIDE.

WAIT. IT COLLAPSED BECAUSE IT WAS *COVERED BY LAVA.*

THAT CAN'T BE SAFE TO EXPLORE!

OH, STOP WORRYING. IT'S JUST A BUNCH OF ROCKS. THEIR TREASURE ROOM WAS BURIED, SO THEY HAD TO BLAST A TUNNEL INTO THE LAVA TO GET THEIR TREASURE OUT. DOESN'T THAT SOUND COOL?

MIGHTYCLAWS TOLD ME ABOUT IT LAST NIGHT.

THERE!

EEEEP.

HOW DID THEY DIE?

MY GUESS IS THEY GOT CAUGHT HERE DURING THE ERUPTION AND NO ONE COULD GET TO THEM UNTIL THE LAVA COOLED.

HOW INCREDIBLY AWFUL.

I WONDER WHAT I'D DO WITH A PILE OF TREASURE...

UNLESS IT COULD STOP THE WAR OR GET ME BACK TO MY FRIENDS, IT'D BE USELESS TO ME.

MAYBE WE SHOULD GO.

I THINK SO. I DON'T KNOW HOW MUCH AIR IS DOWN HERE, BUT I DON'T WANT TO FIND OUT BY RUNNING OUT.

YIKES! THAT'S ALL YOU HAD TO SAY!

DID I SEE SOMETHING—?

A DREAMVISITOR!

I ALWAYS THOUGHT BEING A NIGHTWING MEANT YOU WANTED TO BE AWAKE ALL NIGHT. I CAN NEVER WAKE UP IN THE MORNING, BUT ONCE IT'S DARK, I'M FULL OF ENERGY! DOES THAT HAPPEN TO YOU? MAYBE MY FRIENDS ARE RIGHT AND I'M JUST WEIRD.

ACCORDING TO THE SCROLLS, A DREAMVISITOR CAN BE USED TO VISIT OTHER DRAGONS IN THEIR DREAMS.

OR EVEN TO SEE AND HEAR WHAT'S GOING ON AROUND THEM, IF THEY'RE IN A SHALLOW SLEEP WITH NO DREAMS.

GOOD NIGHT.

GMPHOOD NIGHMPHT.

OKAY... BRING ME TO SUNNY!

NO? ...OKAY, HOW ABOUT GLORY? ...CLAY? ...TSUNAMI?

ARGH. *NOTHING.*

MAYBE THEY'RE AWAKE. WHO ELSE CAN I...

TRY A RAINWING. THEY'RE ALWAYS ASLEEP.

KINKAJOU?

WHHHOOOOOOOSSSH

JUST—CONVINCE THEM? A BUNCH OF STRANGE SKYWING SOLDIERS?

SO INSTEAD OF US KILLING THEM, WE'RE ASKING THEM TO KILL US!

I FORESEE THAT THIS IS GOING TO GO REALLY, REALLY BADLY!

ME TOO! MAYBE I HAVE MAGIC NIGHTWING POWERS, TOO!

THEY'RE GOING TO KILL ME! SKYWINGS AND SEAWINGS ARE ENEMIES!

NOT IF YOU'RE CONVINCING. GO!

FATESPEAKER, YOU STAY.

WE'LL SEE HOW WELL STARFLIGHT DOES THIS TIME.

IF QUEEN RUBY SAYS WE... BACK TO THE PALACE, I'M GOING...

QUEEN SCARLET... ALIVE. SHE'LL KILL US IF WE ABANDON...

...SO WHERE IS SHE? WHAT KIND OF QUEEN LEAVES...

IT'S *NOT* CHAOS. WE HAVE RUBY NOW. AND SHE SAYS...

QUEEN *BURN* SAYS...

SHE'S NOT *OUR* QUEEN!

THAT'S *ENOUGH!* NO ONE'S GOING ANYWHERE TODAY. NOT IN *THIS* STORM. WE'LL DISCUSS IT AGAIN TOMORROW.

USELESS!

PERHAPS NOT, FLAME.

SOME OF THEM ARE CLEARLY DISSATISFIED WITH BURN. IF SHE'S TRYING TO ACT LIKE THEIR QUEEN NOW THAT SCARLET IS GONE, A LOT OF SKYWINGS MIGHT NOT LIKE IT, AND WE CAN USE THAT.

FANCY TALK. NOW LET'S SEE YOU ACTUALLY DO IT.

KNOCK! KNOCK!

WOW, DRAGONS ACTUALLY CALL US THAT? UGH! I HEREBY FORBID ANYONE TO USE THAT PHRASE AGAIN.

IS THAT A ROASTED SEAGULL? ANYONE GOING TO FINISH THAT?

CHOMP
NOM NOM

SAY SOMETHING, STARFLIGHT!

WHY CAN'T I SPEAK?

WHIMPER

AFTER YOU ESCAPED—WHY COME BACK?

TO *HERE*, OF ALL PLACES?

AND WHAT DID YOU DO TO THE SEAWINGS? NO ONE'S HEARD FROM THEM SINCE THE ATTACK ON THE SUMMER PALACE.

DO *YOU* HAVE QUEEN SCARLET? WHERE *IS* SHE?

NONE OF THAT MATTERS.

WE'RE HERE TO TELL YOU YOU'RE SUPPORTING THE WRONG SANDWING. BURN ISN'T GOING TO BE QUEEN. LIKE THE PROPHECY SAYS, SHE'S GOING TO DIE.

*WE'VE* CHOSEN BLISTER.

HOW *DARE* YOU?

TRAITOR!

BLISTER KILLED MY BROTHER!

WE'RE NOT TAKING ORDERS FROM PUNY DRAGONETS!

HER FATE IS TO DIE BENEATH MY TALONS!

BUT YOU *HAVE* TO LISTEN TO US!

WE'RE THE DRAGONETS FROM THE PROPHECY!

NO. YOU'RE NOT.

I WAS STATIONED AT THE QUEEN'S PALACE WHEN THEY WERE THERE, AND THIS IS *NOT* THE SEAWING WE CAPTURED. THE ONE WE CAPTURED WAS *FEMALE*. AND *BLUE*. AND *FEROCIOUS*— SHE LEFT THESE SCARS ON MY NECK.

THIS SNIVELING CREA-TURE IS NO DRAGONET OF DESTINY.

LET'S KILL HIM. PERHAPS WE SHOULD KILL THEM ALL.

NO!

I *AM* THE NIGHTWING THE QUEEN HELD PRISONER. I SWEAR!

REMEMBER, SHE HAD ME FIGHT SCAVENGERS?

PLEASE BELIEVE ME!

IF YOU'RE THE NIGHTWING FROM THE PALACE, WHERE'S THE SEAWING WHO WAS WITH YOU?

SHE'S GATHERING AN ARMY.

WE'RE GOING TO STOP THIS WAR.

SOON YOU CAN ALL GO BACK TO YOUR FAMILIES. SOON YOU WILL BE SAFE.

SOON THERE WILL BE *PEACE*.

LOOK AT THEIR FACES! THEY DO WANT PEACE.

EVEN AMONG THE FIERCE, BAD-TEMPERED SKYWINGS...

ORDINARY DRAGONS WANT PEACE.

WAS THAT A PROPHECY?

NO. IT WAS A PROMISE.

BUT WHAT ABOUT BLISTER? HAVE YOU REALLY CHOSEN *HER*?

THEY WANT ME TO CONVINCE EVERYONE BLISTER'S DESTINED TO WIN AND THERE'S NOTHING WE CAN DO ABOUT IT.

THOSE TWO SHOULD BE EXECUTED AS SOON AS POSSIBLE.

BUT I *CAN'T* HELP BLISTER BE THE NEXT SANDWING QUEEN.

NO. WE, UM. WE HAVEN'T CHOSEN ANYONE YET.

BUT BURN IS TERRIBLE, TOO, AND YOU MUST KNOW THAT.

LET'S TAKE THEM ALL BACK TO THE PALACE. WE'LL GET THE TRUTH OUT OF THEM.

OH NO...

LEAVE OR I WILL KILL YOU MYSELF.

I NEVER WANT TO SEE YOU AGAIN.

A SEAWING ALONE IN SKYWING TERRITORY— POOR SQUID WON'T LAST A DAY.

MAYBE HE'LL BE OKAY. SOMETIMES DRAGONS SURPRISE YOU.

DON'T GET COMFORT-ABLE, STARFLIGHT. YOU'RE RUNNING OUT OF CHANCES TO SHOW ME YOU CAN OBEY ORDERS.

NOW BACK TO THE ISLAND.

CLAY, LOOK AT ALL THE SCROLLS! I BET EVERYTHING WE NEED TO KNOW IS IN HERE.

REALLY? I DON'T REMEMBER THE PROPHECY SAYING "A BUNCH OF SCROLLS ARE COMING TO SAVE THE DAY."

SEE? ALL THE ANSWERS!

How to Free Rainwing Prisoners

IT'S BLANK... OH NO...

HERE'S WHAT I NEED.

SECRETS OF THE NIGHTWINGS

ARRGH!

SIGH... I KNOW THIS ONE'S BLANK.

HOW TO TELL SUNNY YOU LOVE HER

STARFLIGHT, COME ON!

HURRY, HE'S GOING SOMEWHERE.

THAT POOR RAINWING.

WHAT ARE YOU DOING HERE?

FOLLOWING YOU. WHAT ARE YOU UP TO?

NONE OF YOUR BUSINESS. GO AWAY.

WHAT IF A GUARD CATCHES YOU? YOU'LL BE IN MORE TROUBLE ALONE THAN YOU WOULD BE WITH TWO NIGHTWINGS.

WHATEVER. DO WHAT YOU WANT.

HELLO, SKYWING. GLAD TO SEE YOU ON THE OUTSIDE OF THE BARS.

AND HELLO, STAR-FLIGHT. I DON'T THINK I KNOW YOUR FRIEND.

WHO IS THIS?

THIS IS DEATHBRINGER. HE'S AN ASSASSIN.

HE WAS SENT TO KILL MY FRIENDS, BUT INSTEAD HE LET US GO AND FREED GLORY FROM THE NIGHTWINGS.

KEEP YOUR VOICE DOWN! I *THINK* I'M THE ONLY DRAGON DOWN HERE, APART FROM QUEEN SPLENDOR, BUT YOU NEVER KNOW.

THAT'S QUEEN SPLENDOR?

THE FIRST RAINWING CAPTURED.

THE *IDEA* WAS, ONCE WE HAD THEIR QUEEN, THEY'D DO WHATEVER WE WANTED.

LITTLE DID WE KNOW THAT NOT ONLY DO RAINWINGS HAVE MULTIPLE QUEENS, APPARENTLY THEY CAN GO FOR *MONTHS* WITHOUT NOTICING ONE'S MISSING.

DOESN'T SURPRISE *ME*.

THAT'S ALL GOING TO CHANGE.

BECAUSE OF GLORY?

OH.

IS THAT WHAT *MY* FACE LOOKS LIKE WHEN I THINK OF SUNNY?

YES.

FORGET GLORY! DEATHBRINGER, I NEED TO KNOW HOW TO BECOME AN ASSASSIN.

YOU MEAN, YOU WANT TO KNOW THE BEST WAY TO KILL A DRAGON AND NOT CARE?

YES!

YOU HAVE TO BE DOING IT FOR A REASON YOU BELIEVE IN *COMPLETELY.*

YOU SHOULD ALSO AVOID TALKING TO YOUR TARGETS. IN CASE YOU FIND THEY'RE BEAUTIFUL, SARCASTIC, AND FASCINATING.

IS THAT WHY YOU'RE IN HERE?

PERHAPS.

BUT IT'S NOT A BAD THING TO QUESTION YOUR ORDERS, IF YOU ASK ME.

I'M GOING BACK TO BED. THIS IS *POINTLESS.*

JUST—REMEMBER YOU DON'T *HAVE* TO DO WHAT YOU'RE TOLD. YOU CAN ASK QUESTIONS.

SO I CAN WIND UP LIKE *YOU?* BEHIND BARS, SOON TO BE DUMPED INTO LAVA? *GREAT* ADVICE.

IT COULD BE WORSE.

STARFLIGHT, DID GLORY MAKE IT BACK TO THE RAINFOREST?

YES. BUT SHE'S PRETTY MAD ABOUT ALL THE IMPRISONED RAINWINGS.

OF COURSE SHE IS. I NEVER THOUGHT THAT WAS A GOOD IDEA, FOR THE RECORD.

YOU DON'T—UM, YOU DON'T SEEM...

LIKE A TYPICAL ASSASSIN?

ONCE I WAS TRAINED, I WAS SENT TO THE CONTINENT AND... WELL, ON MY OWN FOR SO LONG, I GUESS I STARTED THINKING MY OWN THOUGHTS. IT MAKES ME QUITE A DISAPPOINTMENT TO THE QUEEN.

YOU'VE MET THE QUEEN?

NO, NOT FACE-TO-FACE, OF COURSE.

AS LONG AS I'VE BEEN ALIVE, SHE WATCHES THROUGH SCREENS AND SPEAKS THROUGH HER DAUGHTER, GREATNESS.

WE NEED TO SPEAK TO HER. HOW CAN WE FIND HER?

NO, NO. LISTEN, IT'S NOT SAFE TO SEEK OUT THE QUEEN. SHE WOULDN'T LIKE IT.

WE DON'T HAVE TO INVADE HER PRIVACY. DOES SHE HAVE A THRONE ROOM?

QUEEN BATTLEWINNER? WE *REALLY* NEED TO TALK TO YOU.

IT'S US, THE DRAGONETS OF DESTINY.

WELL, THE TWO NIGHTWING OPTIONS.

HELLO?

I DON'T THINK THERE'S ANYONE THERE.

THAT IS SO *FRUSTRATING!* YOUR MAJESTY! I'M *NOT* IMPRESSED!

WELL, IT *IS* THE MIDDLE OF THE NIGHT. SHE MUST SLEEP SOMETIME.

ALL RIGHT. WE'LL TRY AGAIN TOMORROW.

SCRAAAAAAAPE

UM... THAT SOUND CAME FROM BEHIND THE WALL.

YOUR MAJESTY?

THEY'RE ALL OVER THE MAP. THERE'S EVEN ONE IN THE ICE KINGDOM.

SCAVENGERS? LIKE THE ONE WHO KILLED QUEEN OASIS AND STARTED THE WAR IN THE FIRST PLACE?

EXACTLY.

SO THESE DENS—THAT'S WHERE THEY LIVE?

I GUESS. I HAVE NO IDEA WHY THE NIGHTWINGS WOULD BE INTERESTED IN THEM.

I'VE ALWAYS IMAGINED THEY LIVED IN HIDDEN DENS, LIKE WARRENS. THE SCROLLS SAY THEY PREFER TO LIVE IN GROUPS LIKE MEERKATS, BUT—

STARFLIGHT! *LOOK!*

THERE'S A TUNNEL!

HAS SHE BEEN UNDER THE LAVA *THIS WHOLE TIME?* THAT'S *NOT POSSIBLE* AND NOW I'M DEFINITELY ABSOLUTELY ONE HUNDRED PERCENT GOING TO DIE BECAUSE

*THAT IS A DRAGON WHO LIVES IN LAVA.*

*STARFLIGHT, STARFLIGHT, STARFLIGHT, DO SOMETHING!!!*

LIKE *WHAT?*

WHO?

US? UH, N-N-N-NO ONE.

PLEASE DON'T KILL US!

DON'T MAKE ME.

HOW?

HOW... DID WE FIND YOU? WE WERE LOOKING FOR THE QUEEN... QUEEN BATTLEWINNER.

I. YOU?

I'M FATESPEAKER AND THIS IS STARFLIGHT. WE—WE'RE THE DRAGONETS FROM THE PROPHECY.

AH.

HMM.

UNIMPRESSIVE.

WHY AREN'T YOU *DEAD*? THE TEMPERATURE—I SAW VENGEANCE'S SCALES—THE PHYSICAL REACTION OF LAVA AND SCALES—IT JUST *ISN'T POSSIBLE!*

EVEN DRAGONS BORN FROM BLOOD-RED EGGS COULD ONLY WITHSTAND THAT HEAT A MINUTE OR TWO—AND NIGHTWINGS DON'T HAVE EGGS LIKE THAT, ANYWAY, SO—THIS *CAN'T* BE HAPPENING!

UM. SCIENTIFICALLY SPEAKING.

*MASTERMIND'S SON.*

SNORT!

STARFLIGHT, STARFLIGHT, THIS WASN'T IN ANY OF MY VISIONS!

THREE MOONS! FATESPEAKER, *LOOK!*

YOU CAN SEE RIGHT DOWN HER THROAT—AND IT'S *BLUE!*

WHAT IS IT?

ICE.

ICE? BUT HOW WOULD...

ICEWINGS! THEIR WEAPON—THE FROSTBREATH!

YOU GOT BLASTED BY AN ICEWING, DIDN'T YOU? IT BREATHED DOWN YOUR THROAT.

YOU WOULD HAVE DIED, BUT...

NOT SO EASY.

GLORY!

DOES SHE STILL THINK I'M A TRAITOR? WILL SHE EVEN LISTEN TO ME?

GLORY?

OH, WOW. THIS IS REAL. YOU FOUND A DREAMVISITOR.

I DIDN'T RUN OFF, GLORY, I SWEAR. THE NIGHTWINGS TOOK ME. I NEVER WOULD HAVE LEFT YOU ALL.

MORROWSEER IS—IS TESTING ME—TO SEE IF I'M WORTHY OF THE PROPHECY—

HE HAS THESE OTHER DRAGONETS HE WANTS TO USE INSTEAD, ONLY HE NEEDS A SEAWING—

SO TSUNAMI'S IN DANGER AND I HAD TO WARN YOU—

STARFLIGHT, STOP! TELL ME EVERYTHING. FROM THE BEGINNING.

UP!

YESTERDAY WAS STUPENDOUSLY UNIMPRESSIVE.

I WANT YOU TO BE ABLE TO FIGHT YOUR WAY OUT OF THAT KIND OF SITUATION NEXT TIME.

SO, TODAY: BATTLE TRAINING.

NEXT TIME? AS IF I'D EVER DO THAT AGAIN!

IF YOU'D RATHER FLY YOURSELF BACK TO THE TALONS OF PEACE, TOO, THERE'S THE EXIT.

MY THROAT HURTS.

THERE'S WATER BACK THERE. CATCH UP AS FAST AS YOU CAN.

COUGH
COUGH

SKYWING, YOU'RE NOT ALLOWED TO DIE. WE'RE GOING TO THE HEALERS.

THE REST OF YOU, STAY OUT OF MY WAY OR YOU'LL BE JOINING VIPER.

NOW WE'RE GOING TO HAVE TO USE THAT STUNTED SANDWING...

HE MEANS SUNNY!

I HAVE TO USE THE DREAMVISITOR TO WARN HER AS SOON AS I CAN.

IF NO ONE CARES WHAT I'M DOING, I'M GOING TO FIND SOME DECENT PREY.

IF THERE IS ANY ON THIS STUPID ISLAND.

LET'S GO TO THE DORMITORY AND REST.

HOW CAN I...

ACTUALLY, SLEEPING SOUNDS LIKE THE ONLY THING I COULD DO RIGHT NOW.

ALTHOUGH I'M AFRAID IT'LL BE NOTHING BUT NIGHTMARES.

I LIKE HOW YOU TURNED OUT.

YOU TOO. I LIKE YOU BETTER THAN ALL THE NIGHTWINGS I'VE MET WHO WERE RAISED "PROPERLY."

I THINK WE'RE BOTH REALLY LUCKY THAT WE DIDN'T HAVE TO GROW UP HERE.

AND I'M THE LUCKIEST OF ALL, GROWING UP WITH DRAGONETS LIKE MY FRIENDS, INSTEAD OF THE ONES POOR FATESPEAKER GOT.

YOU HAVE THE FACE THAT YOU GET WHEN YOU'RE MISSING YOUR FRIENDS.

SOMETIMES I THINK THERE ARE NO OTHER DRAGONS LIKE THEM IN PYRRHIA.

SIGH...

YOU'RE PROBABLY RIGHT.

EXCEPT YOU, FATESPEAKER.

GET SOME SLEEP.

AS SOON AS SHE'S ASLEEP, I'LL USE THE DREAMVISITOR...

STARFLIGHT?

EEK!

MORROWSEER SAID I'D PROBABLY FIND YOU HERE. I'M IN A BIT OF A CONUNDRUM AND HOPING YOU CAN HELP ME.

UH—

HOW CAN I GET OUT OF THIS? I NEED TO DREAMVISIT MY FRIENDS.

WALK WITH ME. HAVE YOU SEEN OUR MARVELOUS LIBRARY?

SORRY, SUNNY. I'LL WARN YOU AS SOON AS I CAN.

THERE'S SOMETHING ABOUT THE SMELL OF SCROLLS THAT ALWAYS CALMS ME, SON.

ME TOO.

MEDICAL RECORDS, MEDICAL RECORDS.

HELP ME BRAIN-STORM. THE QUEEN IS VERY ANGRY ABOUT WHAT HAPPENED TO THE SKYWING DRAGONET. I'M AFRAID HE'LL BE DEAD BY MORNING IF WE CAN'T COUNTERACT THE SANDWING POISON.

WHICH IS APPARENTLY *MY* RESPONSIBILITY FOR SOME REASON, AS IF I'M NOT ALREADY SWAMPED TRYING TO PRODUCE VENOM-PROOF HELMETS FOR THE ENTIRE NIGHTWING TRIBE IN TWO DAYS USING ONLY MY INSUFFICIENTLY TESTED PROTOTYPE, WHICH THE QUEEN SAYS WILL SIMPLY HAVE TO DO FOR NOW.

WAIT. DID YOU SAY TWO DAYS?

IN CASE WE DECIDE TO ATTACK. I TOLD THEM MY RESEARCH IS INCOMPLETE AND I CAN'T GUARANTEE IT WILL GO SMOOTHLY.

THE PROBLEM IS I'VE NEVER *STUDIED* SANDWING VENOM. BUT IF IT'S ANYTHING LIKE RAINWING VENOM, THERE'S NOTHING THAT CAN COUNTERACT IT.

HE HASN'T FIGURED OUT THAT A RELATIVE'S VENOM IS THE ANTIDOTE FOR RAINWING VENOM?

IF ALL THE RAINWINGS MANAGED TO KEEP THAT SECRET, MAYBE THEY'RE TOUGHER AND SMARTER THAN ANYONE THINKS.

NIGHTWINGS KEEP THEMSELVES ISOLATED TO SEEM MORE POWERFUL, BUT IT MEANS THEY'RE CUT OFF FROM SO MUCH KNOWLEDGE. IF THEY DIDN'T FEEL SO SUPERIOR TO OTHER DRAGONS, MAYBE THEY'D LEARN SOMETHING NEW.

UNLIKELY... TRIED THAT ON RAINWING VENOM, DIDN'T WORK...

NONE NEARBY... DOUBTFUL...

FOR NIGHTWING *EYES ONLY!*

WELL?
ANY THOUGHTS?

WE COULD TRY TO REACH OUT AND ASK BLISTER, BUT I'M NOT SURE IT'S ADVISABLE TO GIVE HER ANY POWER OVER US.

SHOULD I TELL THEM ABOUT THE CACTUS CURE FOR SANDWING VENOM?

I DON'T WANT TO HELP THEM, BUT MORE IMPORTANTLY, I DON'T WANT FLAME TO DIE.

SUNNY WOULD SAY SAVE FLAME, DON'T WORRY ABOUT CONSEQUENCES.

TSUNAMI WOULD SAY: "STOP DITHERING!"

FINE. I'LL DO WHAT SUNNY WOULD DO.

MASTERMIND! COME TO THE COUNCIL IMMEDIATELY!

161

THAT MUST BE THE CAVE WHERE THE TUNNEL IS.

I JUST HOPE THEY HAVEN'T HEARD YET ABOUT THE PLANNED ATTACK TONIGHT.

BE CONFIDENT. ACT LIKE WE'RE DOING EXACTLY WHAT WE'RE SUPPOSED TO BE DOING.

NOT A PROBLEM. I MEAN, WE *ARE*.

WHAT IS THE MEANING OF THIS?

HERE WE GO!

DIDN'T YOU GET THE MESSAGE? I *KNEW* THIS WOULD HAPPEN.

THIS IS ONE OF THE DRAGONETS OF THE PROPHECY! AS YOU CAN SEE, HE WAS SLASHED BY A SANDWING TAIL. THE QUEEN ORDERED US TO TAKE HIM THROUGH THE RAINFOREST TO BE HEALED.

UH-HUH. WHY WOULD SHE SEND *YOU?*

SHE SAID I'M THE ONLY NIGHTWING WHO CAN DO IT, BECAUSE THE RAIN-WINGS THINK I'M ON *THEIR* SIDE.

I'LL HAVE TO VERIFY THIS ORDER.

OF *COURSE* YOU DO. I *TOLD* THEM TO SEND A MESSENGER AHEAD OF US.

BUT NO ONE LISTENS TO ME. NOW THE SKYWING'S GOING TO *DIE* BECAUSE WE'RE DELAYED! THE QUEEN IS GOING TO BE *FURIOUS!*

GASP!

OOF!

EW!

NO! HE CAN'T DIE! HE'S THE *ONLY* SKYWING WE'VE GOT! IF HE DIES, THAT MEANS NO *PROPHECY,* NO *PLAN,* NO *RAINFOREST HOME* FOR OUR TRIBE!

BUT THIS SOLDIER IS RIGHT, HE DOES HAVE TO VERIFY THE ORDER. WHY, WE MIGHT—WE MIGHT—

WAIT, WHAT *ARE* YOU WORRIED WE'LL DO?

WELL... I DON'T KNOW.

WE'VE *GOT* TO LET THEM GO THROUGH, CHIEF! THE QUEEN IS RIGHT—HE'S THE ONLY ONE WHO CAN GET INTO THE RAINFOREST. HE CAN GET THE SKYWING TO THE CURE.

...ALL RIGHT.

BUT NO FUNNY BUSINESS. FIX THE SKYWING AND COME BACK.

WE'LL BE BACK BY NIGHTFALL.

TSUNAMI, I HAVE TO SEE GLORY RIGHT *NOW*. THE NIGHTWINGS ARE ATTACKING *TONIGHT*.

GASP!

SHE'LL TAKE YOU TO THE QUEEN.

CLAY AND I HAVE TO STAY ON GUARD HERE. RAINWINGS, IT TURNS OUT, HAVE A TENDENCY TO FALL ASLEEP. EVEN ON *IMPORTANT ASSIGNMENTS*.

SURE.

BUT IF THERE'S ANY BATTLE PLANNING, I WANT TO BE INVOLVED!

OF COURSE.

BE CAREFUL.

I'M READY FOR THEM. DON'T WORRY.

NOM

NOM

I NEVER THOUGHT OF IT THAT WAY.

*YOUR* SCALES ARE A GREAT COLOR. ALL THE SANDWINGS I'VE MET ARE SORT OF PALE AND DUSTY-LOOKING.

I KNOW, I'M WEIRD.

YOU'RE THE ALTERNATE NIGHTWING, RIGHT? GLORY SAID STARFLIGHT HAD LOTS OF NICE THINGS TO SAY ABOUT YOU.

*REALLY?* SUCH AS WHAT? SPECIFICALLY?

WHAT WAS IT LIKE GROWING UP IN THE TALONS OF PEACE CAMP?

BIZARRE. WE WERE ALWAYS MOVING SO NO ONE COULD FIND US.

BUT IT MUST HAVE BEEN AMAZING TO LIVE WITH SO MANY DRAGONS FROM DIFFERENT TRIBES!

YES! I WAS ALWAYS TRYING TO FIGURE OUT WHICH TRIBE I WAS MOST LIKE, BUT—

AS STRANGELY ADORABLE AS YOU TWO ARE, I NEED YOU TO EITHER GO DISCOVER YOUR TWIN SOULS ELSEWHERE, OR FOCUS ON BATTLE PLANNING WITH ME.

BATTLE PLANNING.

MANGROVE, GRANDEUR, THANKS FOR COMING.

LET'S TAKE THIS MEETING TO THE TUNNEL. I NEED TSUNAMI AND CLAY'S INPUT, TOO.

...SO AT LEAST SOME OF THEM ARE AFRAID OF US.

I'D SAY MOST OF THEM. THEY'RE TERRIFIED OF YOUR VENOM.

THEY SHOULD BE.

YOURS, MAYBE. BUT THE REST OF THE RAINWINGS... I'M NOT SURE THEY'LL USE IT EVEN IN A LIFE-OR-DEATH SITUATION. IT'S HARD TO CHANGE AN ENTIRE TRIBE'S PHILOSOPHY IN THREE DAYS.

I'M NOT SURE WE SHOULD CHANGE IT, TSUNAMI. I LIKE THEIR PHILOSOPHY.

I COULD DO IT. FOR THE SAKE OF MY TRIBE. BUT THE OTHERS WOULD HAVE TROUBLE.

BUT I MEANT, DO YOU WANT TO STAY HERE BECAUSE WE'RE GOING TO FIGHT YOUR TRIBE? IF IT'S TOO MUCH TO ASK, I UNDERSTAND.

THEY'RE *NOT* MY TRIBE. *YOU* ARE.

YOU AND SUNNY AND TSUNAMI AND CLAY.

AW, YOU BIG SAP.

I'VE GOT TO PREPARE THE FIRST WAVE. LET'S GO CHANGE THE WORLD.

I MIGHT DIE TODAY.

WHAT IF I DIE WITHOUT EVER TELLING HER HOW I FEEL?

YOU'VE BLUFFED NIGHT-WING GUARDS. YOU'VE ESCAPED THE NIGHTWING ISLAND.

SURELY YOU CAN SAY THREE WORDS TO ONE DRAGON.

STARFLIGHT, WE'RE GOING TO BE ALL RIGHT.

THINK OF THE PROPHECY. WE *HAVE* TO BE ALIVE TO STOP THE WAR, RIGHT? SO WE *CAN'T* DIE TODAY.

ISN'T THAT COMFORTING?

I WISH I HAD YOUR OPTIMISM.

IT'S NOT OPTIMISM. IT'S FAITH. THERE'S A REASON WE'RE HERE.

SUNNY, THERE'S SOMETHING I'VE NEEDED TO TELL YOU... FOR A LONG TIME, I MEAN.

I'M LISTENING.

I LOVE YOU.

I CAN'T BELIEVE YOU'RE REALLY HERE.

DO YOU FEEL THE EARTH SHAKING?

THAT'S ME. ALL THE HAPPINESS INSIDE US IS TRYING TO BURST OUT.

ACTUALLY, I *THINK* THAT WAS AN EARTHQUAKE...

GRANDEUR, LIANA, DISGUISE YOURSELVES AS NIGHTWINGS AND GO TO THE OTHER CAVES. SHOW EVERYONE HOW TO FREE THE PRISONERS, THEN GET BACK TO THE TUNNEL.

THE MOST IMPORTANT THING IS GETTING ALL FOURTEEN PRISONERS HOME SAFE.

MANGROVE AND ORCHID, CALM YOUR SCALES DOWN AND THEN HEAD BACK TO THE RAINFOREST.

I SHOULD COME WITH YOU. YOU'LL NEED—

WE'VE GONE THROUGH A LOT OF TROUBLE TO REUNITE YOU AND ORCHID.

SOMEBODY ELSE CAN GO WITH ME.

FATESPEAKER, STARFLIGHT, COME ON.

LET'S GO HAVE A TALK WITH THE NIGHTWING QUEEN.

PLEASE TELL ME THERE'S AN INVISIBLE ARMY WITH US.

I'M YOUR INVISIBLE ARMY.

I'M SERIOUS! WE SHOULDN'T GO IN WITH JUST THE THREE OF US.

THE DUNGEONS YOU SAW— HOW DO WE GET THEM OPEN? WILL THOSE SPEARS WORK, OR DO WE NEED KEYS?

KEYS, I THINK.

SO LET'S START WITH THE QUEEN. WE'LL MAKE HER TELL US WHERE THE KEYS ARE.

WOW, THIS IS AN IMPRESSIVE MAP.

WHAT ARE YOU DOING IN HERE?

PRINCESS GREATNESS!

UH, WE... GOT LOST?

THAT'S HOW THE QUEEN PLANS TO GET TO THE RAINFOREST. MY FATHER IS MAKING HER A PORTABLE LAVA DEVICE.

HOW WOULD IT STAY HOT AWAY FROM THE VOLCANO? CAN ANY METAL REALLY CONTAIN IT?

PREPARATIONS?

EVERYONE'S GATHERING. BUT, MOTHER, I CAN'T LEAD THEM INTO BATTLE MYSELF. CAN'T WE POSTPONE? MASTERMIND SAYS YOUR ARMOR ISN'T READY...

IT WILL BE. TONIGHT.

I'M AFRAID I DON'T THINK SO. I NEED MORE TIME TO MAKE SURE THIS WILL WORK.

TONIGHT, MASTERMIND. I CAN'T TRUST *HER* TO RUN THE INVASION.

YOU *SHOULDN'T!* I DON'T KNOW WHAT TO DO. SO I WAS COMING TO ASK YOU, AND THEN—

THEN SHE RAN INTO ME.

AND YOU ARE?

QUEEN GLORY OF THE RAINWINGS. I'VE COME TO GIVE YOU ONE CHANCE TO END THIS WAR BEFORE WE DESTROY YOU.

FUNNY.

IF YOU THINK AN ICEWING ATTACK IS HARD TO LIVE WITH, TRY RAINWING VENOM. YOUR LAVA BATH WON'T HELP WITH THAT.

HIISSSSSSSSSSSSSSSSSSS

BUT *ONLY* IF THEY ALL SWEAR TO ACCEPT *YOU* AS THEIR NEW QUEEN.

WHAT?

A NEW HOME FOR THE NIGHTWINGS, SAFE AND PEACEFUL, AND ALL THEY HAVE TO DO IS GIVE UP THEIR CRUELTY AND VIOLENCE AND OBEY YOU.

HMM.

NEVER!

MOTHER, IT SOUNDS LIKE A GOOD PLAN TO ME.

YOU'RE A *PATHETIC HEIR.*

RUUUUUUUUUUUUUUUUUUMBLE

I KNOW I AM. BEING QUEEN IS AWFUL.

BUT—WHAT ABOUT OUR REAL QUEEN?

SHE KNOWS SHE'S NOT MAKING IT TO THE RAINFOREST. THERE'S NOTHING YOU CAN BUILD THAT WILL KEEP HER ALIVE THERE.

SHE'S GOING TO DIE HERE, CRUSHED BY THE VOLCANO ALONG WITH THE NIGHTWING HOME. AND IF SHE WANTS HER TRIBE TO SURVIVE, SHE'S GOT TO HAND THEM OVER TO QUEEN GLORY.

I AM *THEIR* QUEEN. I AM!

WAIT, STARFLIGHT. I HAVEN'T AGREED TO THIS. I DON'T SEE HOW WE COULD TRUST THE NIGHTWINGS IN OUR FOREST.

THESE DRAGONS HAVE BEEN ABDUCTING AND TORTURING MY TRIBE. HOW CAN WE JUST FORGIVE THEM?

WE HAVE TO GET OUT OF HERE!

BBBRRRRRRRRRRK-K-KKK-TT

KKKKRRR KK KKK RRR

WHERE ARE THE DUNGEONS?

KKRRRCK RRRRRRR KKK KRK

THERE'S NO TIME!

WE ARE *NOT* LEAVING DEATHBRINGER!

RRRRRUUUUUUMMMMBBLE

FATESPEAKER, POINT ME TOWARD THE DUNGEONS. STARFLIGHT, GET EVERY ONE OFF THE ISLAND.

THEY'RE THAT WAY.

I CAN'T LET HER GO BY HERSELF.

GREATNESS! WHERE ARE THE KEYS TO THE DUNGEON PRISONS?

TH-TH-THERE'S A SET HIDDEN IN THE COAL NICHE AT THE BOTTOM OF THE DUNGEON STAIRS.

WHAT ABOUT THE VOLCANO? ARE WE ALL GOING TO DIE?

TAKE FATESPEAKER TO THE GREAT HALL AND TELL ALL THE NIGHTWINGS OUR TERMS. IF THEY'LL SWEAR LOYALTY TO QUEEN GLORY, BRING THEM TO THE TUNNEL. IF NOT, THEY'D BETTER FLY FOR THE CONTINENT AS FAST AS THEY CAN.

RRRRRUUUUUUMMMMBLE

BUT GLORY DIDN'T SAY YES!

I'LL TALK HER INTO IT! GO!

THIS WAY!

WE'RE HERE TO RESCUE YOU. YOU'RE GOING HOME!

WAIT HERE.

WHAT? WHY AREN'T WE *LEAVING?!*

KKKKRRRRRTTT KKK

WRONG KEY...

YOU DON'T HAVE TO DO THIS.

OH, I DON'T? THAT'LL SAVE ME SOME TIME. GOOD LUCK WITH THE VOLCANO.

C'MON, C'MON.

THAT'S IT! COME ON!

RRRRUUUMMMBLE

KKK KT KT

KRRRREEEEK    KKKKKRRRRRAAACK

KK KRRRRRT

KKKKKRRRRRRAAAAAAACI

THIS WAY!

KKKRRRT KRRRAAAAACK KRRAACK

OCHRE! I DIDN'T EVEN THINK TO LOOK FOR HIM.

IS... EVERYONE LEAVING? I'M... NOT SURE WHAT'S HAPPENING. SOMEONE SAID BANANAS THIS WAY?

JUST FOLLOW THE OTHERS INTO THE TUNNEL. WE'LL EXPLAIN LATER.

RRRRUUUUUMMMMBBLLEE

STARFLIGHT, THIS DRAGON WANTED TO TALK TO YOU.

OH. CLAY, THIS IS MASTERMIND. MY... MY FATHER.

RRRRUUUUUMMMMBBLLEE

IT, UH, IT OCCURS TO ME AT THIS, UH, RATHER INOPPORTUNE JUNCTURE THAT OUR HOSTS MAY, ER, HATE ME.

DO YOU THINK... WILL THEY REALLY LET ME LIVE THERE? AFTER EVERYTHING?

RRRUMMMBLEEEEEE

THEY PROBABLY DO HATE YOU. I THINK THEY SHOULD, DON'T YOU?

BUT—BUT SCIENCE— AND MY ORDERS—AND—

RRRRUUUUUMMMMBBLLEE

DON'T MAKE EXCUSES. WHEN YOU GET THERE, TELL THE QUEEN YOU'RE SORRY, AND TAKE YOUR PUNISHMENT. THAT'S MY ADVICE.

THEN YOU'LL END UP BACK HERE. OR DEAD. EITHER IS FINE WITH ME.

WE MADE YOU. WE CAN *UNMAKE* YOU JUST AS EASILY.

NO, YOU CAN'T. WE HAVE A PROPHECY TO FULFILL, AND THERE'S NOTHING YOU CAN DO TO STOP IT.

*STOP* IT? I'VE BEEN TRYING TO MAKE IT HAPPEN FOR ALMOST TEN YEARS.

PROPHECIES DON'T WORK LIKE THAT. YOU CAN'T CONTROL THEM. WHATEVER IS GOING TO HAPPEN WILL HAPPEN—THAT'S THE WHOLE *POINT* OF DESTINY.

ON THE CONTRARY, I CERTAINLY *CAN* MAKE MY PROPHECY HAPPEN HOWEVER I WANT...

SSSSSHHHHSSSSSSHHHH

...CONSIDERING I'M THE ONE WHO MADE IT UP IN THE FIRST PLACE.

YOU *WHAT?*

WAIT... THE PROPHECY... ISN'T REAL?

THE DRAGONET PROPHECY ISN'T REAL.

YOU'RE JUST SAYING THAT TO BE AWFUL!

SSSSZZZZZZZZ...

QUEEN BATTLEWINNER AND I WROTE IT TOGETHER AFTER THE LAST ERUPTION DESTROYED PART OF THE FORTRESS.

WE KNEW WE'D NEED A NEW HOME SOON.

AND THE PROPHECY WAS OUR PLAN TO GET IT.

WHAT DOES THE PROPHECY HAVE TO DO WITH WHERE THE NIGHTWINGS LIVE?

WE PLANNED TO CONTROL THE DRAGONETS BY INCLUDING A NIGHT-WING WHO, NAT-URALLY, WOULD BE THE LEADER.

WE HAD NO IDEA YOU'D BE SUCH AN *ABYSMAL* FAILURE.

THE NEXT STEP WAS TO CHOOSE A SANDWING QUEEN AND JOIN FORCES TO GUARANTEE SHE'D WIN.

THEN YOUR ALLY, WHOEVER YOU PICKED, WOULD HELP YOU TAKE OVER THE RAINFOREST.

IN THE PROPHECY— "*DARKNESS WILL RISE TO BRING THE LIGHT*"—THAT'S SUPPOSED TO MEAN THE NIGHTWINGS!

EXACTLY. THE ONLY REALLY IMPORTANT PART OF THE PROPHECY.

THE REST OF IT? SMOKE AND MIRRORS.

NO!

THE PROPHECY *IS REAL!*

WE WERE BORN TO END THE WAR AND SAVE EVERYONE!

AFRAID NOT. YOU'RE JUST AS ORDINARY AS ANY DRAGON.

WOW. NO WONDER I'VE ALWAYS *FELT* ORDINARY.

BUT YOU'RE NOT—YOU'RE *NOT* ORDINARY!

WHAT ABOUT THE RED MUDWING EGG? WHAT ABOUT *MY* EGG ALONE IN THE DESERT?

THERE ARE SCIENTIFIC PATTERNS TO THINGS LIKE THE APPEARANCE OF BLOOD EGGS. WE USE THEM IN OUR PROPHECIES TO IMPRESS OUR INFERIORS.

AS FOR THE SANDWING EGG, WE PLANNED TO SET THAT UP, BUT WE GOT A TIP YOURS WAS THERE ALREADY.

A COINCIDENCE.

NO, IT WASN'T! IT WAS *FATE!*

ON THE ONE TALON, MORROWSEER, YOU ARE THE *WORST.*

ON THE OTHER— SUNNY, THINK WHAT THIS MEANS!

WE CAN LIVE OUR OWN LIVES! WE DON'T HAVE TO FOLLOW SOME PLAN THE STARS LAID OUT FOR US!

BUT I *WANT* TO STOP THE WAR! I *LIKE* HAVING A DESTINY!

ALL THOSE DRAGONS OUT THERE WHO BELIEVE IN THE PROPHECY— IN *US*. WHO WILL SAVE THEM?

NO ONE.

THE NIGHTWINGS ARE IN THE RAINFOREST NOW, SO WE HAVE NO REASON TO JOIN THE WAR. IT WILL DRAG ON *ENDLESSLY*...

AND MORE DRAGONS WILL *DIE* EVERY DAY, FOR GENERATIONS, ALL WONDERING ABOUT THE AMAZING DRAGONETS WHO WERE *SUPPOSED* TO SAVE THEM...

BUT—

OBVIOUSLY—

FAILED.

SOB!

SEE YOU IN THE RAINFOREST.

NO!

# EPILOGUE

BLAZE

P-P-PLEASE CAN'T WE GO INSIDE, GLACIER?

NOT YET.

YOU'RE SURE ABOUT WHAT YOU HEARD, BLAZE? THE NIGHTWINGS HAVE ALLIED WITH BLISTER, AND ARE FORCING THE DRAGONETS TO CHOOSE HER?

THAT'S WHAT IT SOUNDED LIKE.

BLISTER

NAUTILUS? WHERE IS MORROWSEER?

FORGIVE MY LATENESS, QUEEN BLISTER.

I-I DON'T KNOW.

WHO IS THAT?

MY SON, SQUID. MORROWSEER LEFT HIM TO DIE, BUT BY A MIRACLE, ONE OF OUR SPIES FOUND HIM.

BURN

ANY WORD ON THE DRAGONETS?

THEY'VE VANISHED AGAIN. THERE'S A RUMOR THAT THEY'RE RESPONSIBLE FOR KILLING ALL THE SKYWINGS AT THE NORTHERNMOST OUTPOST.

IS THAT LIKELY, YOUR MAJESTY?

IN THE ARENA, THEY DIDN'T SEEM VERY FIERCE. BUT THEN THEY ATTACKED SCARLET, SO WHO KNOWS. I WISH I'D GOTTEN MY CLAWS ON ALL THEIR EGGS BEFORE THEY HATCHED.

WE NEED TO DECIDE WHAT TO DO ABOUT THIS PROPHECY.

WE DON'T WANT THE DRAGONETS TELLING ANYONE THEY'VE CHOSEN QUEEN BLISTER. IT WOULD BE VERY DEMORALIZING.

I'M SURE THEY WON'T CHOOSE HER NOW THAT THEY'VE MET ME! NOW THEY KNOW I'M WONDERFUL!

HMMM.

JUST IN CASE, WE SHOULD FIND THESE DRAGONETS. I'D LIKE TO... *CHAT* WITH THEM MYSELF.

I HATE NIGHTWINGS.

I RATHER HATE THEM, TOO.

IF MORROWSEER DOESN'T SHOW UP, I KNOW WHOSE FAULT IT IS. THOSE *DRAGONETS*.

THEY'VE CAUSED TROUBLE FOR THE WRONG DRAGON. I WILL HUNT THEM DOWN, AND THEN—PROPHECY OR NO PROPHECY— I'M GOING TO KILL THEM ALL.

AND RUBY?

THE SUPPOSED NEW QUEEN OF THE SKYWINGS IS A *NUISANCE*. SHE WANTS TO "RESTORE ORDER" IN HER KINGDOM BEFORE JOINING ME IN ANY MORE BATTLES.

IT'S FRUSTRATING. I *REALLY* NEED TO *KILL* SOMETHING.

THERE'S ALWAYS YOUR PRISONER.

TSK, SMOLDER! QUEEN SCARLET IS OUR *GUEST*! UNTIL I DECIDE HOW USEFUL SHE CAN BE.

NO, I HAVE ANOTHER VICTIM IN MIND. OR *FIVE* OF THEM, TO BE EXACT.

SOON WE'LL PUT AN END TO THIS PROPHECY NONSENSE ONCE AND FOR ALL.

**TUI T. SUTHERLAND** is the author of the #1 *New York Times* and *USA Today* bestselling Wings of Fire series, the Menagerie trilogy, and the Pet Trouble series, as well as a contributing author to the bestselling Spirit Animals and Seekers series (as part of the Erin Hunter team). In 2009, she was a two-day champion on *Jeopardy!* She lives in Massachusetts with her wonderful husband, two awesome sons, and two very patient dogs. To learn more about Tui's books, visit her online at www.tuibooks.com.

**BARRY DEUTSCH** is an award-winning cartoonist and the creator of the Hereville series of graphic novels, about yet another troll-fighting 11-year-old Orthodox Jewish girl. He lives in Portland, Oregon, with a variable number of cats and fish.

**MIKE HOLMES** has drawn for the series Secret Coders, Adventure Time, and Bravest Warriors. He created the comic strip True Story, the art project *Mikenesses*, and his work can be seen in *MAD* Magazine. He lives in Philadelphia with his wife Meredith and son Oscar, along with Heidi the dog and Ella the cat.

**MAARTA LAIHO** spends her days and nights as a comic colorist, where her work includes the comics series Lumberjanes, Adventure Time, and The Mighty Zodiac. When she's not doing that, she can be found hoarding houseplants and talking to her cat. She lives in the woods of Maine.